Courage

written by
Zanni Louise

art by
Missy Turner

FIVE MILE

A big heart helps you care for the world, care for yourself, and care for others.

But how do you grow your heart?

One ingredient you can use to grow your heart is courage.

Courage is doing something you find hard.

Jack doesn't like swimming.

He sits on the edge of the pool while his friends splash and play.

'Come in, Jack!' calls Mina.

'I can't,' says Jack.

But it does look so fun.

Jack takes a big breath.
He stands in the shallow end.

Li Wei splashes him.

The water feels good.
Jack takes one step deeper.

Soon, Jack is swimming with his friends.

Courage is stepping towards the thing that frightens you.

Mina wants to talk to the new girl.
But what if the new girl doesn't like her?

All day, Mina watches from a safe distance.

The day is nearly over.

Mina breathes in, and calls out. 'Hello, I'm Mina!'

She's glad she does. Mina and Lucy make gnome homes in the sandpit.

*Courage is trying and messing up.
And trying again!*

Rosie is a jellyfish in the school play.

What if no-one knows what she is?
Even worse, what if she trips on a tentacle?

Her head pounds. She wants to run away.

But she doesn't.

She steps on stage …
and steps on a tentacle!

No-one laughs.

Her mum smiles from the front row. Rosie smiles back.

*Scary things aren't always big.
But they can feel big.*

Lila's library book is due back. But Lila can't find it anywhere!

She knows she has to tell Miss Rachel. What if she gets in trouble?

Lila's legs feel fizzy. But she knows that Miss Rachel is kind. She knows people make mistakes sometimes.

Courage is discovering mistakes are okay.

Jack works hard on his lion.
It's the best lion he's ever drawn.

'Lions don't live at the beach, Jack!' says Lila.

Jack's heart deflates.

But then he has an idea.

Jack gives the lion a suitcase.

'He's on holiday!' Jack tells Lila.

*Sometimes, you want to be courageous.
But it feels too risky.*

'Li Wei, what have you brought for Show and Tell?' asks Miss Rachel.

Li Wei stays quiet. His tummy flips.
He knows he will jumble up the words.

'Li Wei?' Miss Rachel asks again.

Li Wei is bursting to share.
'My rabbit had babies yesterday!' he says at last.

The first branch is safe.
So is the second.

Rosie is nearly as high as Lila.

The world looks so small from up here!

Having the courage to make mistakes helps you find out what you like. And what you are good at.

Mina has always wanted to play violin.
She wishes like crazy it could be easy. But when she tries, the violin sounds like a sick bird.

She tries again.

It squawks rudely.

So Mina decides to have fun.

Playing amazingly is going to take time.

Having the courage to mess up makes you realise you don't need to be perfect.

Li Wei is going to visit his grandparents.
They can't understand English.
And he can't understand Chinese.

So before Li Wei visits, he practises simple sayings in the mirror.

'I am a cake,' Li Wei says in Chinese.

He blushes, realising his mistake.

But Nǎinai smiles, and hands him a *fa gao*. It is delicious!

When you have courage, you get to make new friends ...

and find out what you are good at.

Courage helps you discover you don't need to be perfect,

and that some things feel scary for a reason.

But when we realise we are still safe, and that mistakes are okay, you learn and you grow.

Courage helps your heart grow, so you can look after the world, yourself and each other.

What does courage mean to you?

Let's talk about courage

Can you remember a time when you were courageous?

Yoav circus performer and magician
'I got accepted to a circus school. I was afraid that I wouldn't be good enough, but then I realised that if I want to grow I'd have to step out of my comfort zone. I ended up really enjoying it.'

Denise fashion designer
'It took me five years to gather the courage to start my own label. Fear of failure was holding me back. But when I realised the joy of the journey would far outweigh the risk of failure, I took the plunge.'

Brett musician
'I was really nervous about starting high school. It was so big! I had to catch a bus by myself, and didn't know anyone. But I realised I wasn't the only one who was nervous. Sharing my feelings made me, and others feel better.'

Fritha social entrepreneur
'I knew I needed courage to do something to help my new Indian friend get people into her shop so she could send her kids to school. Even if it takes my whole life to help her and others like her, I'm determined!'

Discussion questions for children

Courage means doing things that are important, even if they are scary. Sometimes we need courage to do the things that keep us healthy, happy and safe.

- Can you think of a time you needed courage?
- What feelings did you get in your body?
- What were some of your worries?
- What did you do that helped you to have courage?
- Who helped you?
- Can you think of some things you would like to do in the future that might need you to be courageous?

Notes for parents and carers

Courage helps us cope with fear so we can do the things that make life meaningful. Children need courage to try new activities, make friends and deal with transitions, such as starting school.

The relationship between you and your child forms the foundation upon which courage is built. When a child is raised in a safe, consistent and loving environment, they will feel more confident to explore the world. When given the space to take risks and make mistakes, they learn that many of the things they fear are not really dangerous. They learn how to solve problems, deal with failure and move through difficult feelings, knowing they have a secure base to return to.

Courage will look different for every child. Some children may take longer to build up their courage. Some may need a little extra support from caregivers.

Explain to your child that it is okay to feel afraid. Fear is just our brain trying to protect us. Sometimes our brain gets it wrong and tells us we are in danger when we are not. This is called anxiety. Anxiety feels uncomfortable, but it does not need to control us. We can learn how to manage anxiety and be brave, so we can keep doing the things that matter to us.

Tips for nurturing courage in children

- Have regular conversations with your child about emotions, and listen to their fears and worries. Some fears may seem small to you, but it is important not to minimise their emotions. Acknowledge their feelings and, if necessary, help them identify solutions.

- When children worry they tend to overestimate the likelihood that something bad will happen and underestimate their ability to cope. Help your child identify the realistic risks and rewards of trying something difficult or new. They will learn that the most challenging tasks are often the most rewarding.

- Ask your child what they are currently unable to do because they feel anxious or fearful of failure. Help them set clear, manageable goals.

- Help your child break big goals into smaller steps. Start with the least difficult steps and move up to the most difficult.

- Support your child through their emotions as they attempt each step. Help them learn strategies to manage anxious feelings, such as slow, steady breathing.

- Accept any feelings that arise and give them the space to keep trying. Resist the urge to rush in and remove your child from the situation or give them lots of reassurance. This might require some courage of your own!

- Praise your child for their efforts and encourage them to keep practising. The more they face their fears, the more their courage will grow.

Dr Ameika Johnson Child Clinical Psychologist

Also available in this book series

Honesty

Honesty is talking to yourself and others truthfully. Honesty brings us closer, keeps us safer and helps people trust us. Honesty is not always easy. Sometimes it's the hardest choice.

There are many ways to be honest ...

Persistence

Persistence is never giving up, even when things get tough. Persistence helps us try new things, get better at hard things, and cope when things get difficult. Persistence helps us see things through to the end.

There are many ways to be persistent ...

Made with love by the team at
FIVE MILE
Alex, Niki, Jade, James, Andy, Amy, Amanda & Caity

Five Mile,
the publishing division
of Regency Media
www.fivemile.com.au

First published 2020

Text copyright © Zanni Louise, 2020
Illustrations copyright © Missy Turner, 2020
Interviews, page 28: Interviewee material copyright © individual interviewees
Psychologist notes, pp 29—31: Psychologist notes copyright © Dr Ameika Johnson, 2020
All rights reserved. No part of this publication may be reproduced, stored in a retrieval system, or transmitted in any way or by any means, electronic, mechanical photocopying, recording or otherwise, without the prior permission of the publisher.

A catalogue record for this book is available from the National Library of Australia

Printed in China 5 4 3 2 1